The Elephant's Child

and other stories

Miles
KeLLy

First published in 2011 by Miles Kelly Publishing Ltd
Harding's Barn, Bardfield End Green, Thaxted, Essex, CM6 3PX, UK

2 4 6 8 10 9 7 5 3 1

Publishing Director Belinda Gallagher

Creative Director Jo Cowan

Editor Amanda Askew

Senior Designer Joe Jones

Production Manager Elizabeth Collins

Reprographics Anthony Cambray, Stephan Davis, Lorraine King, Jennifer Hunt

ISBN 978-1-84810-499-0

Printed in China

British Library Cataloguing-in-Publication Data
A catalogue record for this book is available from the British Library

ACKNOWLEDGEMENTS
Artworks are from the Miles Kelly Artwork Bank

Cover artwork by Rupert van Wyck (Beehive Illustration)

Every effort has been made to acknowledge the source and copyright holder of each picture.
Miles Kelly Publishing apologises for any unintentional errors or omissions.

Made with paper from a sustainable forest
www.mileskelly.net
info@mileskelly.net

www.factsforprojects.com

Contents

The Elephant's Child

From *Just So Stories* by Rudyard Kipling

IN THE HIGH and far-off times, the Elephant, oh best beloved, had no trunk. He had only a blackish, bulgy nose, as big as a boot, that he could wriggle about from side to side; but he couldn't pick up things with it. But there was one Elephant – a new Elephant – an Elephant's Child – who was full of 'satiable curtiosity, and that means he asked ever so many questions. And he lived in Africa, and he filled all Africa with his 'satiable curtiosities. He asked his tall aunt, the Ostrich, why her tail feathers grew just so, and his tall aunt the Ostrich spanked him with her hard, hard claw.

He asked his broad aunt, the Hippopotamus, why her eyes were red, and his broad aunt, the

Hippopotamus, spanked him with her broad, broad hoof; and he asked his hairy uncle, the Baboon, why melons tasted just so, and his hairy uncle, the Baboon, spanked him with his hairy, hairy paw. And still he was full of 'satiable curtiosity! He asked questions about everything that he saw, or heard, or felt, or smelt, or touched, and all his uncles and his aunts spanked him. And still he was full of 'satiable curtiosity!

One fine morning in the middle of the Precession of the Equinoxes this 'satiable Elephant's Child asked a new fine question that he had never asked before. He asked, "What does the Crocodile have for dinner?"

Then everybody said, "Hush!" in a loud and dreadful tone, and they spanked him immediately and directly, without stopping, for a long time.

By and by, when that was finished, he came upon Kolokolo Bird sitting in the middle of a wait-a-bit thorn-bush, and he said, "My father has spanked me, and my mother has spanked me; all my aunts and uncles have spanked me for my 'satiable curtiosity; and still I want to know what the Crocodile has for dinner!"

Then Kolokolo Bird said, with a mournful cry, "Go to the banks of the great grey-green, greasy Limpopo River, all set about with fever-trees, and find out."

That very next morning, when there was nothing

left of the Equinoxes, because the Precession had preceded according to precedent, this 'satiable Elephant's Child took a hundred pounds of bananas (the little short red kind), and a hundred pounds of sugar-cane (the long purple kind), and seventeen melons (the greeny-crackly kind), and said to all his dear families, "Goodbye. I am going to the great grey-green, greasy Limpopo River, all set about with fever-trees, to find out what the Crocodile has for dinner." And they all spanked him once more for luck, though he asked them most politely to stop.

Then he went away, a little warm, but not at all astonished, eating melons, and throwing the rind about, because he could not pick it up.

He went from Graham's Town to Kimberley, and from Kimberley to Khama's Country, and from Khama's Country he went east by north, eating melons all the time, till at last he came to the banks of the great grey-green, greasy Limpopo River, all set about with fever-trees, precisely as Kolokolo Bird had said.

Now you must know and understand, Oh Best Beloved, that till that very week, and day, and hour, and minute, this 'satiable Elephant's Child had never seen a Crocodile, and did not know what one was like. It was all his 'satiable curtiosity.

The first thing that he found was a Bi-Coloured-Python-Rock-Snake curled round a rock.

"'Scuse me," said the Elephant's Child most politely, "but have you seen such a thing as a Crocodile in these promiscuous parts?"

"Have I seen a Crocodile?" said the Bi-Coloured-Python-Rock-Snake, in a voice of dreadful scorn. "What will you ask me next?"

"'Scuse me," said the Elephant's Child, "but could you kindly tell me what he has for dinner?"

Then the Bi-Coloured-Python-Rock-Snake uncoiled himself very quickly from the rock, and spanked the Elephant's Child with his scalesome, flailsome tail.

"That is odd," said the Elephant's Child, "because my father and my mother, and my uncle and my aunt, not to mention my other aunt, the Hippopotamus, and my other uncle, the Baboon, have all spanked me for my 'satiable curtiosity – and I suppose this is the same.

So he said goodbye very politely to the Bi-Coloured-Python-Rock-Snake, and helped to coil him up on the rock again, and went on, a little warm, but not at all astonished, eating melons, and throwing the rind about, because he could not pick it up, till he trod on what he thought was a log of wood at the very edge of the great grey-green, greasy Limpopo River, all set about with fever-trees.

But it was really the Crocodile, Oh Best Beloved, and the Crocodile winked one eye – like this!

"'Scuse me," said the Elephant's Child most politely, "but do you happen to have seen a Crocodile in these promiscuous parts?"

Then the Crocodile winked the other eye, and lifted half his tail out of the mud; and the Elephant's Child stepped back most politely, because he did not wish to be spanked again.

"Come hither, Little One," said the Crocodile. "Why do you ask such things?"

"'Scuse me," said the Elephant's Child most politely, "but my father has spanked me, my mother has spanked me, not to mention my tall aunt, the Ostrich, and my tall uncle, the Giraffe, who can kick ever so hard, as well as my broad aunt, the Hippopotamus, and my hairy uncle, the Baboon, and including the

Bi-Coloured-Python-Rock-Snake, with the scalesome, flailsome tail, just up the bank, who spanks harder than any of them; and so, if it's quite all the same to you, I don't want to be spanked any more."

"Come hither, Little One," said the Crocodile, "for I am the Crocodile," and he wept crocodile-tears to show it was quite true.

Then the Elephant's Child grew all breathless, and panted, and kneeled down on the bank and said, "You are the very person I have been looking for all these long days. Will you please tell me what you have for dinner?"

"Come hither, Little One," said the Crocodile, "and I'll whisper."

Then the Elephant's Child put his head down close to the Crocodile's musky, tusky mouth, and the Crocodile caught him by his little nose, which up to that very week, day, hour, and minute, had been no bigger than a boot, though much more useful.

"I think," said the Crocodile – and he said it between his teeth, like this – "I think today I will begin with Elephant's Child!"

At this, Oh Best Beloved, the Elephant's Child was much annoyed, and he said, speaking through his nose, like this, "Led go! You are hurtig be!"

Then the Bi-Coloured-Python-Rock-Snake scuffled down from the bank and said, "My young friend, if you do not now, immediately and instantly, pull as hard as ever you can, it is my opinion that your acquaintance in the large-pattern leather ulster" (and by this he meant the Crocodile) "will jerk you into yonder limpid stream before you can say Jack Robinson."

Then the Elephant's Child sat back on his little haunches, and pulled, and pulled, and pulled, and his nose began to stretch. And the Crocodile floundered into the water, making it all creamy with great sweeps of his tail, and he pulled, and pulled, and pulled.

And the Elephant's Child's nose kept on stretching; and the Elephant's Child spread all his little four legs and pulled, and pulled, and pulled, and his nose kept on stretching; and the Crocodile threshed his tail like an oar, and he pulled, and pulled, and pulled, and at each pull the Elephant's Child's nose grew longer and longer – and it hurt him terribly!

Then the Elephant's Child felt his legs slipping, and he said through his nose, which was now nearly five feet long, "This is too butch for be!"

Then the Bi-Coloured-Python-Rock-Snake came down from the bank, and knotted himself in a double-clove-hitch round the Elephant's Child's hind legs. And he pulled, and the Elephant's Child pulled, and the Crocodile pulled; but the Elephant's Child and the Bi-Coloured-Python-Rock-Snake pulled hardest; and at last the Crocodile let go of the Elephant's Child's nose with a plop that you could hear all up and down the Limpopo.

Then the Elephant's Child sat down most hard and

sudden; but first he was careful to say "Thank you" to the Bi-Coloured-Python-Rock-Snake; and next he was kind to his poor pulled nose, and wrapped it all up in cool banana leaves, and hung it in the great grey-green, greasy Limpopo to cool.

"What are you doing that for?" said the Bi-Coloured-Python-Rock-Snake.

"'Scuse me," said the Elephant's Child, "but my nose is badly out of shape, and I am waiting for it to shrink.

"Then you will have to wait a long time, said the Bi-Coloured-Python-Rock-Snake. "Some people do not know what is good for them."

The Elephant's Child sat there for three days waiting for his nose to shrink. But it never grew any shorter, and, besides, it made him squint. For, Oh Best Beloved, you will see and understand that the Crocodile had pulled it out into a really truly trunk, same as all Elephants have today.

At the end of the third day a fly came and stung him on the shoulder, and before he knew what he was doing he lifted up his trunk and hit that fly dead with the end of it.

"'Vantage number one!" said the Bi-Coloured-Python-Rock-Snake. "You couldn't have done that with a mere-smear nose. Try and eat a little now."

Before he thought what he was doing the Elephant's Child put out his trunk and plucked a large bundle of grass, dusted it clean against his fore-legs, and stuffed it into his own mouth.

"Vantage number two!" said the Bi-Coloured-Python-Rock-Snake. "You couldn't have done that with a mear-smear nose. Don't you think the sun is hot?"

"It is," said the Elephant's Child, and before he thought what he was doing he schlooped up a schloop of mud from the banks of the great Limpopo, and slapped it on his head, where it made a cool schloopy-sloshy mud-cap all trickly behind his ears.

"Vantage number three!" said the Bi-Coloured-Python-Rock-Snake. "You couldn't have done that with a mere-smear nose. Now how do you feel about being spanked again?"

"'Scuse me," said the Elephant's Child, "but I should not like it at all."

"How would you like to spank somebody?" said the Bi- Coloured-Python-Rock-Snake.

"I should like it very much indeed," said the Elephant's Child.

"Well," said the Bi-Coloured-Python-Rock-Snake, "you will find that new nose of yours very useful to spank people with."

"Thank you," said the Elephant's Child, "I'll remember that; and now I think I'll go home to all my dear families and try."

So the Elephant's Child went home across Africa frisking and whisking his trunk. When he wanted fruit to eat he pulled fruit down from a tree, instead of waiting for it to fall as he used to do. When he wanted grass he plucked grass up from the ground, instead of going on his knees as he used to do. When the flies bit him he broke off the branch of a tree and used it as fly-whisk; and he made himself a new, cool, slushy-squishy mud-cap whenever the sun was hot. When he felt lonely walking through Africa he sang to himself down his trunk, and the noise was louder than several brass bands. He went especially out of his way to find a broad Hippopotamus (she was no relation of his), and he spanked her very hard, to make sure that the Bi-Coloured-Python-Rock-Snake had spoken the truth about his new trunk. The rest of the time he picked up the melon rinds that he had dropped on his way to the Limpopo – for he was a Tidy Pachyderm.

One evening he came back to all his dear families, and he coiled up his trunk and said, "How do you do?" They were glad to see him, and said, "Come here and be spanked for your 'satiable curtiosity."

"Pooh," said the Elephant's Child. "I don't think you peoples know anything about spanking; but I do, and I'll show you." Then he uncurled his trunk and knocked two of his dear brothers head over heels.

"Oh Bananas!" said they, "where did you learn that trick, and what have you done to your nose?"

"I got a new one from the Crocodile on the banks of the great grey-green, greasy Limpopo River," said the Elephant's Child.

"It looks very ugly," said his hairy uncle, the Baboon.

"It does," said the Elephant's Child. "But it's very useful," and he picked up his hairy uncle, the Baboon, by one hairy leg, and hove him into a hornet's nest.

Then that bad Elephant's Child spanked all his dear families for a long time. He pulled out his tall Ostrich aunt's tail feathers; and he caught his tall uncle, the Giraffe, and dragged him through a thorn-bush; and he shouted at his aunt, the Hippopotamus, and blew bubbles in her ear when she was sleeping in the water.

At last, his dear families went off one by one to the banks of the great Limpopo River to borrow new noses from the Crocodile. When they came back nobody spanked anybody any more; and ever since that day, all the Elephants have trunks precisely like the trunk of the 'satiable Elephant's Child.

Eva's Visit to Fairyland

By Louisa M Alcott

DOWN AMONG THE grass and fragrant clover lay little Eva by the brook-side, watching the bright waves, as they went singing by under the drooping flowers that grew on its banks. As she was wondering where the waters went, she heard a faint sound. She thought it was the wind, but not a leaf was stirring, and soon through the rippling water came a strange little boat.

It was a lily of the valley, whose tall stem formed the mast, while the broad leaves that rose from the roots, and drooped again till they reached the water, were filled with fairies, who danced to the music of the silver lily-bells above that rang a merry peal, and filled the air with their fragrant breath.

On came the fairy boat till it reached a rock, and here it stopped, while the fairies rested beneath the violet leaves, and sang with the dancing waves.

Eva looked with wonder and threw crimson fruit for the little folks to feast upon.

They looked kindly on the child, and, after whispering long among themselves, two elves flew over the shining water, and, lighting on the clover blossoms, said gently, "Little maiden, many thanks for your kindness, our queen bids us ask if you will go with us to Fairyland, and learn what we can teach you."

"I would go with you, dear fairies," said Eva, "but I cannot sail in your little boat. See! I can hold you in my hand, and could not live among you without harming your tiny kingdom, I am so large."

Then the elves laughed, saying, "You are a good child to fear doing harm to those weaker than yourself. Look in the water and see what we have done."

Eva looked into the brook, and saw a tiny child standing between the elves. "Now I can go with you," said she, "but I can no longer step from the bank to yonder stone, for the brook seems now like a great river, and you have not given me wings like yours."

But the fairies took each a hand, and flew lightly over the stream. The queen and her subjects came to meet her. "Now must we go home," said the queen, "and you shall go with us, little one."

Then there was a great bustle, as they flew about on shining wings, some laying cushions of violet leaves in the boat, others folding the queen's veil and mantle more closely round her.

The cool waves' gentle splashing against the boat, and the sweet chime of the lily-bells, lulled little Eva to sleep, and when she woke it was in Fairyland. A faint, rosy light, as of the setting sun, shone on the white pillars of the queen's palace as they passed in. They led

Eva to a bed of pure white leaves, above which drooped the fragrant petals of a crimson rose.

With the sun rose the fairies, and, with Eva, hastened away to the gardens, and soon, high up among the tree-tops, or under the broad leaves, sat the elves in little groups, taking their breakfast of fruit and pure fresh dew.

"Now, Eva," said they, "you will see that Fairies are not idle spirits. Come, we will show you what we do."

They led her to a lovely room, through whose walls of deep green leaves the light stole softly in. Here lay many wounded insects, and creatures, and pale, drooping flowers grew beside urns of healing herbs, from whose fresh leaves came a faint, sweet perfume.

Eva wondered, but silently followed her guide, little Rose-Leaf, who went to the insects – first to a little fly who lay in a flower-leaf cradle.

"Do you suffer much, dear Gauzy-Wing?" asked the Fairy. "I will bind up your poor little leg." So she folded the cool leaves tenderly about the poor fly, bathed his wings, and brought him refreshing drink, while he hummed his thanks, and forgot his pain.

They passed on, and Eva saw beside each bed a fairy, who with gentle hands and loving words soothed the suffering insects.

Then Rose-Leaf led Eva away, saying, "Come now to the Flower Palace, and see the Fairy Court."

Beneath green arches, bright with birds and flowers, went Eva into a lofty hall. Suddenly the music grew louder and sweeter, and the fairies knelt, and bowed their heads, as on through the crowd of loving subjects came the queen, while the air was filled with gay voices singing to welcome her.

She placed the child beside her, saying, "Little Eva, you shall see now how the flowers on your great earth bloom so brightly. A band of loving little gardeners go daily forth from Fairyland, to tend and watch them. Now, Eglantine, what have you to tell us of your rosy namesakes on the earth?"

From a group of elves, whose rose-wreathed wands showed the flower they loved, came one bearing a tiny urn, and, answering the queen, she said:

"Over hill and valley they are blooming fresh and fair as summer sun and dew, and this have I brought to place among the fairy flowers that never pass away." Eglantine laid the urn before the queen, and placed the fragrant rose on the dewy moss beside the throne, while a murmur of approval went through the hall, as each wand waved to the little fairy who could bring so fair a gift to their good queen.

Said little Rose-Leaf to Eva, "Come now and see where we are taught to read the tales written on flower-leaves, and the sweet language of the birds, and all that can make a fairy heart wiser and better."

Then into a cheerful place they went, where were many groups of flowers, among whose leaves sat the child elves, and learned from their flower-books all that fairy hands had written there. Some studied how to watch the tender buds – when to spread them to the sunlight, and when to shelter them from rain, how to guard the ripening seeds, and when to lay them in the warm earth or send them on the summer wind to far off hills and valleys, where other fairy hands would tend and cherish them. Others learned to heal the wounded insects, who, were it not for fairy hands, would die before half their happy summer life had gone. Eva nodded to the little ones, as they peeped from among the leaves at the stranger, and then she listened to the fairy lessons. Several tiny elves sat on leaves while the teacher sat among the petals of a flower beside them, and asked questions that none but fairies would care to know.

At last, Eva said farewell to the child elves, and hastened with little Rose-Leaf to the gates. Here she saw many bands of fairies, folded in dark mantles that mortals might not know them, who, with the child among them, flew away over hill and valley. Some went to the cottages amid the hills, some to the seaside to watch above the humble fisher folks, but little Rose-Leaf and many others went into the noisy city.

Eva soon learned that the fairy band went among the poor and friendless, bringing pleasant dreams to the sick and old, sweet, tender thoughts of love and gentleness to the young, strength to the weak, and patient cheerfulness to the poor and lonely.

After their work was done, they turned towards

Fairyland, which was dressed in flowers, and the soft wind went singing by, laden with their fragrant breath. Sweet music sounded through the air, and troops of elves in their gayest robes hastened to the palace where the feast was spread.

Soon the hall was filled with smiling faces and fair forms, and little Eva, as she stood beside the queen, thought she had never seen a sight so lovely.

Long they feasted, gaily they sang, and Eva, dancing merrily among them, longed to be an elf that she might dwell forever in so fair a home.

At length the music ceased, and the queen said, as she laid her hand on little Eva's shining hair: "Dear child, tomorrow we must bear you home, therefore we will guide you to the brook-side, and there say farewell till you come again to visit us."

On a rosy morning cloud, went Eva through the sunny sky. The fresh wind bore them gently on, and soon they stood again beside the brook, whose waves danced brightly as if to welcome them.

"Now, we say farewell," said the queen, as they gathered nearer to the child.

They clung about her tenderly, and little Rose-Leaf placed a flower crown on her head, whispering softly, "When you would come to us again, stand by the brook-side and wave this in the air, and we will gladly take you to our home again. Farewell, dear Eva. Think of your little Rose-Leaf when among the flowers."

For a long time Eva watched their shining wings, and listened to the music of their voices as they flew singing home. When at last little form had vanished among the clouds, she saw that all around her, the fairest flowers had sprung up.

The Firebird

A Russian folk tale

LONG AGO IN RUSSIA, there lived a lord called Tsar Andronovich who owned a magnificent garden. At the centre of the garden lay a beautiful orchard, and in the middle of the orchard grew Tsar Andronovich's favourite tree – a tree that grew golden apples. No one was allowed to touch the golden apple tree except for Tsar Andronovich himself. But one night, an amazing firebird with wings of flame and eyes of crystal came blazing into the orchard and stole some of the fruit.

"A fortune to whoever brings me this amazing firebird alive." Tsar Andronovich declared the very next day. "This creature is even more splendid than the golden apples she has been stealing!"

Half an hour later, the Tsar's three sons galloped out of the gates in search of the firebird. The eldest and middle son, Dimitri and Vassili, thundered off together. The youngest son, Ivan, went off sadly on his own.

Ivan rode for three days. His food began to run low, and his horse was exhausted. Just as Ivan thought things couldn't get much worse, he heard a howl and out of a dark forest ran a grey wolf. Ivan's horse shot away, throwing him into the dirt. But it didn't escape far. The wolf sprang onto it and gobbled it up.

"Eat me quickly!" Ivan cried at the panting beast.

"I am not going to eat you," grinned the wolf. "I have to repay you for eating your horse. Ride on me and I will take you where you want to go."

Ivan was too tired and lonely to argue. He climbed onto the grey wolf's back and explained all about his quest to find the firebird. He had hardly finished speaking when the grey wolf leapt away like an arrow. It seemed only a few seconds before they halted at a stone wall.

"Ivan, climb this wall and you will see the firebird in a golden cage," the wolf explained. "Take the firebird, but whatever you do, do not steal the golden cage."

Trembling, Ivan clambered over the wall and found himself in a courtyard below. Hanging from a tree was a golden cage with the firebird inside, just as the wolf had said. Ivan crept over to it, opened the jewelled door, and drew out the beautiful firebird. 'I really need the cage as well,' thought Ivan. He reached up and unhooked the cage. At that moment, ear-splitting alarm bells rang and guards rushed in from all sides. They dragged Ivan to their master, Tsar Dolmat.

"You must pay dearly for trying to steal my precious firebird," boomed Tsar Dolmat, his face dark with anger. Then he rubbed his beard and thought for a second. "UNLESS," he added, "you go to the ends of the earth and bring me the horse with the golden mane. If you do this, I will give you the firebird with pleasure."

Ivan crept back to the grey wolf in shame. But his friend simply said, "Ride on me and I will take you where you want to go."

The grey wolf sprang away faster than the wind. It seemed only a couple of minutes before they stopped outside some stables.

"Ivan, go into these stables and take the horse with the golden mane," the wolf told him. "But whatever you do, do not steal its golden bridle."

Cautiously, Ivan edged into the stables, crept up to the horse with the golden mane, and began to lead it out of its stall. 'I really need the bridle as well,' thought Ivan. He lifted down the bridle and a clanging peal of bells broke the silence. Soldiers dashed into the stable and hauled Ivan away to see their master, Tsar Afron.

"You must pay dearly for trying to steal my wonderful horse with the golden mane," raged Tsar Afron, shaking with fury. "UNLESS," he added, "you go to the other side of the world and bring me Tasha the Beautiful to be my bride. If you do this, I will gladly give you the horse with the golden mane."

When Ivan returned empty-handed, the wolf did not scold. He simply said, "Ride on me and I will take you where you want to go."

Ivan jumped onto the grey wolf and he sped away to the other side of the world as quick as lightning. It seemed only an hour before they drew up outside a glorious palace.

"Ivan, this time I am going to be the one who goes inside and you are going to be the one who waits," said the wolf and he sprang over the palace wall with one mighty bound. Ivan hardly had time to draw breath before the wolf came springing over again – this time with Tasha the Beautiful tossed onto his back. Ivan leapt onto the wolf and they were off through the air like a shooting star.

By the time the three arrived back at Tsar Afron's home, the grey wolf was highly surprised to find Ivan weeping bitterly.

"Why are you crying?" the grey wolf asked.

"I have fallen in love with Tasha," Ivan protested, "and she has fallen in love with me. I cannot let her go."

The grey wolf looked at Tasha the Beautiful and she nodded sadly.

"Oh very well," sighed the grey wolf. "I will turn myself into the form of Tasha the Beautiful. You can present me to Tsar Afron in her place and he will give you the horse with the golden mane. When you are two mountains away, think of me and I will be back at your side."

And so, Tsar Afron was tricked and soon Ivan was once again mounted on the grey wolf while his sweetheart, Tasha the Beautiful, rode on the horse with the golden mane.

As they drew near the villa of Tsar Dolmat, Ivan sighed a deep sigh. "Oh grey wolf," he began, "I would so like to keep this horse with the golden mane. Would you turn into the form of the horse, as you disguised yourself as Tasha before? Then I could take you to Tsar Dolmat and win the firebird. When I am two forests away, I will think of you and you will return back to my side."

The grey wolf looked at Ivan and bowed slightly.

"For you, I will do this." And so it came to pass and Tsar Dolmat was tricked. Ivan once again mounted the grey wolf while his sweetheart, Tasha the Beautiful, rode on the horse with the golden mane and carried the firebird.

By and by, the companions came to the very spot where the grey wolf had set upon Ivan's horse and eaten it. Then it was the grey wolf's turn to sigh a deep sigh. "Well, Ivan, here I took a horse from you and here I now return you with another horse, a beautiful bride and a firebird, too! You no longer need me and I must go." And with that, the grey wolf disappeared into the woods.

Ivan and Tasha went on their way in sadness, weeping for their lost friend. As they stopped to rest, the two figures of Dimitri and Vassily crept out of the shadows. They had returned from their travels empty-handed and were enraged to find their little brother not only with the firebird, but also with Tasha the Beautiful. In their bitterness, the brothers drew their swords and stabbed Ivan where he lay, dreaming. Then they swept up Tasha the Beautiful and the firebird, and were off to their father's mansion to pretend that the treasures were theirs. "Breathe a word of this and we'll kill you, too," they hissed into Tasha's ear, making her shake with sorrow and fear.

Ivan's body lay lifeless and cold. Snow began to cover him like a thick blanket. Birds and woodland creatures slowly crept closer to find out what was lying so silent and still in the freezing weather – and among them came a grey wolf with yellow eyes and drooling jaws. He stalked right up to Ivan's body and sniffed all around. Throwing his head back, he gave a spine-chilling howl. Slowly and gently, the wolf began to lick the wound in Ivan's chest. And suddenly, Ivan sat up and began to shiver.

"Why am I asleep in this snowstorm?" he asked the grey wolf.

"Ride on me," came the gruff voice, "and I will take you where you want to go."

"Home," whispered Ivan into his friend's ear, "I want to go home." And no sooner had he finished saying the words than they were there.

Of course, when Tsar Andronovich learnt the truth, he threw the wicked Dimitri and Vassily in a dungeon.

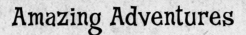

Ivan and Tasha the Beautiful were married – Ivan rode his faithful grey wolf to the wedding and Tasha arrived on the horse with the golden mane. As for Tsar Andronovich, well, he got his precious firebird after all – and he loved her so much, he even let her eat the golden apples from his favourite tree whenever she wanted.

Thumbelina

Retold from the original tale
by Hans Christian Andersen

ONCE UPON A TIME there was a woman who wanted more than anything in the world to have a child – but she didn't know where to get one. She went to see a witch about it and the witch gave her a special seed. The woman planted the seed in a flowerpot and it grew into a bud that looked very much like the bud of a tulip. "What a beautiful flower!" the woman murmured one day, and she leant over and kissed the closed petals. POP! the bud exploded into an open flower, and sitting in the middle of it was a tiny little girl, no bigger than the woman's thumb.

The woman was overjoyed with her beautiful daughter and named her Thumbelina. The woman thought that her tiny daughter was utterly delightful and looked after her tenderly. But one night, a big, fat toad came hopping through a broken pane of glass in the woman's window. 'Hmmm', thought the toad, as her bulging eyes caught sight of Thumbelina sleeping in half a walnut shell. 'She would make a perfect wife for my son'. The toad picked up the dreaming little girl, and hopped away to the marshy river where she lived. The toad placed Thumbelina on a broad, flat lily pad. 'Now you can't run away', the toad thought, and she swam off to break the good news to her son...

When Thumbelina woke up and saw that she was not only lost, but trapped too, she began to cry bitterly. The fish wiggled up to see what was causing all the tiny splashes and ripples, and they took pity on the sad, tiny girl. Quickly and silently, they nibbled through the lily pad's green stem and Thumbelina went floating down the river. Soon, she was far out of the toads' reach...

and still the lily pad raft floated on. Thumbelina sailed past towns and was swept out into the countryside. Thumbelina liked it among the fields. It was sunny and peaceful, and a pretty white butterfly fluttered down to keep her company. Suddenly a large flying beetle dive-bombed the lily pad and wrapped his legs around Thumbelina's tiny waist. In a flash, Thumbelina found herself sitting on a twig with the beetle high up in a tree, watching her lilypad drift away without her.

Hundreds of the beetle's curious friends came crawling out of the bark to peer at what he had brought home. "Urgh! Look, it's only got two legs," the beetle children squealed.

"Where are its feelers?" some of the lady beetles murmured.

"Hasn't it got a slim bottom?" other lady beetles gasped in horror, admiring their own round shiny ones.

"It is ugly," the male beetles had to admit. "Let's get rid of it." And they flew down from the tree with Thumbelina and sat her on a daisy.

Poor Thumbelina felt very like crying. But just then she noticed a little hole in the earth below her that looked very like it was a type of doorway. She jumped down from the daisy and peered into the gloom.

"Hello!" she cried. "Is anyone at home?"

After a few seconds, out popped a fieldmouse's head. She looked Thumbelina up and down, and tutted loudly. "Dear, dear!" the fieldmouse scolded. "You look exhausted and hungry. If you're as lost as you look, you're very welcome to stay here with me – in return for keeping my rooms nice and clean and tidy."

So all winter Thumbelina lived with the fieldmouse. Every day, she washed and swept and scoured and polished, and the fieldmouse was very kind to her. Although, truth to tell, Thumbelina found life rather boring. The fieldmouse wasn't at all skilled at making conversation and neither was her regular visitor, Mr Mole. He came once every week in his fine black velvet overcoat, but he didn't like to talk. He just enjoyed sitting and peering at Thumbelina through his little eyes, listening to her sing.

The fieldmouse was delighted that her friend so liked Thumbelina. "I think he's falling in love with you," she whispered to Thumbelina excitedly.

The fieldmouse was even more sure that she was right when Mr Mole invited them both to visit him in his splendid underground mansion.

"I have dug a tunnel from your house to mine," Mr Mole informed them, "so you may come and see me in comfort. Only please close your eyes when you are halfway down the passage, for I am afraid that a dead swallow is lying there."

Thumbelina wasn't at all revolted when she came across the dead bird on her first trip to Mr Mole's house. Instead, she felt pity for the poor thing, lying all stiff and still on the cold earth. While the fieldmouse ran on eagerly ahead, Thumbelina bent down and stroked the bird's feathers. "Goodbye, sweet swallow," she murmured, and she laid her head on the bird's soft breast. DUP! DUP! DUP! Thumbelina heard the swallow's heart beating – only very faintly, but Thumbelina knew that the bird was still just alive!

From then on, Thumbelina found as many excuses as possible to creep away from the fieldmouse and into the tunnel to care for the swallow.

Gradually the swallow began to recover. By the time the weather had begun to grow warmer, the swallow was well enough to stand and hop about. On the first day of spring, the swallow was totally better.

"One day, I will repay you," he twittered as he hopped up the passageway and soared off into the sky.

It was then that the fieldmouse announced to Thumbelina that she had arranged for her to be married to Mr Mole. "He is very wealthy and will take good care of you," the fieldmouse beamed.

But Thumbelina was horrified. "I cannot live my life underground!" she cried, and ran sobbing out into the fields. Just then, Thumbelina heard a familiar twittering above her head. She looked up and saw her friend the swallow swooping down towards her. "Come away with me," cried the swallow, "I know a place where you will be happy."

Joyfully, Thumbelina jumped onto his back.

The swallow flew off with Thumbelina to a land where the weather was always sunny, and where in every flower there lived a tiny person just like Thumbelina. Thumbelina was very happy in her new home. She even married a handsome prince who lived in a rosebud and who was extremely glad that she had never become Mrs Mole!